Little Cry Babys

Don't Let The Bully Win

By: Rayvell Vann

ISBN-1 ISBN: 9798824768275

Printed in the USA

Dedication

This book is dedicated to my 3 daughters Marquita , Gianna, and Raynya my loving moms Azline and Bertha my sisters Ericka, Trina, Lil Val , Nibbie ,lady, Monda, the twins Yvette and Yvonne Tisa, Tyris, Therisa, Shanny, Shanetta my brothers Darnell, (Earl R.I.P) all my nieces and nephews especially Walter you're one of a kind nephew to all my friends especially Tasha Holland this wouldn't be possible without you. I love you dearly Chrystol, you know Imma always love you and Dominique, (Nikki) you 'll always be in my heart. To my grandson Chase, I love you. Pig and Misti it's still way outta order, my Aunt Boo, you're the best cook ever. Cousin Charmz, I learned a lot from you for anyone that I forgot stop it I didn't. Shout out to Derrace Butler.

In Loving Memory of Mable McDonald

Today a new student, named Patty Jakes is introduced by Ms. Tasha to the kids in in the class. While Spanky made a fat joke about Patty's weight.

1

Kids let's welcome our new student PATTY JAKES
Hello
WHAT'S UP
Hello
Did she say FATTY J CAKES?
DOG YOU NEED HELP
2

While EricKA AND PAtty we're
going to lunch TAe AND QUA
Also KNOWN As the (spoiled
bratt Girlz) stArt tAlKiNg
About PAtty As they wAlK
by.

Girl I'm o.K I got Bullied At My other Schools thats why I'm Here. I WAS Hoping this School would be different
Look AT the 2 FAT ugly crew
Don't worry About tHem tHeY Are ReAL HATERS
I BET SHe SMells BAd

While eating in the cafeteria
Ericka notice that Patty is
not eating her lunch and
Patty tell her why she is not
eating

How come you're not eating Patty?
Girl I'm trying to loose a few pounds because I'm tired of the fat girl jokes about me. How do you handle the fat boy jokes Spanky?
I don't.. I'm skinnyly challenged not fat. Now are you going to eat them cookies and fries?

Someone has put a pork sub
sandwich on Patty's locker
with a note that read "you
are what you eat piggy"
Kids are laughing at Patty
as she run away crying.

WHo did THis? THis is NOT FUNNY
LOOK YA'LL iT'S A PORK SANDWICH ON FATTYS LOCKER HA HA HA
SHE'S SO FAT, SHE'S CAUSIN' A LITTLE EARTHQUAKE HA HA HA
PORK
YOU ARE WHAT YOU EAT PIGGY
8

PAtty is crying iN the girl's looker rooM While ERicKA is beiNg A good frieNd to her.

I'M TIRED of BEING NICE TO EVERYONE ONLY to be bullied, because of MY WEIGHT. I HATE LIVING, SOMETIMES I WISH I WE'RE...
SNIFF SNIFF
STOP IT PATTY DON'T SAY THAT AND STOP CRYING NO BODY SHOULD EVER PICK ON ANYONE SOME PEOPLE ARE JUST NOT NICE. THEY NEED HELP! NOT YOU LOVE YOURSELF FIRST.
10.

Charmz, David, Carlito and
Spanky are in the hallway
talking about what had
happend to Patty today.

MAN did you guys HEAR ABOUT WHAT THEM CLOWNS did to PATTY?
Football Tryou
MAN THEY did HER WRONG
THAT NOT COOL
TODAY
OH I bet iT WAS TAG AND QUA UGLY SELFS LETS go ge SOME ICECREAM
S
7
12

The spoiled Bratt Girlz Are
cracking jokes on charmz
carlito and spanky

13

SHUT UP YOU MONKEY MOUTH TROLLS
YA'LL SO UGLY
TALK TO THE HAND

TAE AND QUA lied ON
CArlito AND told Ms. TAShA
thAt he put the PorK Sub
SANdwich oN PAtty's locKer
Now Ms, TAShA has put
him iN Time aJT for A Hour.

15

BECAUSE QUA AND TAE LIED ON ME. THEY SAID THAT I PUT THE SANDWICH ON PATTY'S LOCKER.
THEIR WILD WITH THEIR STYLE I CAN'T STAND THEM
HOW COME YOU'RE IN TIME OUT HOMIE?
TIME OUT
WOW
L.O.S
?
S
16

CHARMZ, SPANKY. AND ERICKA
ASK COACH O'NEAl for help
About how to stop A bully
ERICKA AlSO Tell HiM About
WHAt HAd HAPPENd To PATTY
yesterday. The COACH do Not
REAlize just how Much Words
CAN hurt people.

First off she need to do a few thousand sit ups and table push backs boycott snacks. You too Spanky. Don't worry kids will be kids
Coach what can we do about them bullying Patty?

18

the Kids ARe SAd, becAuse They
JUst found out that PATTY had
committed Suicide LAst Night,
becAuse She WAS SICK ANd
tiRed of being the victim
of Bullies.

"PATTY'S LAST POST ONLINE WAS "I'M TIRED OF BEING BULLIED ANYMORE, CHANGING SCHOOLS EVERY FEW MONTHS. NO ONE WILL EVER HURT MY FEELINGS AGAIN goodbye cruel cruel world"
DANG SHE'S GONE
THAT'S SAD
I'M GOING TO MISS HER, WE COULD HAVE HELPED HER
I HATE BULLIES

MIS. TASHA reAds the letter that
PATTY left behind.

Dear Everybody,
          I'm sorry that I
could not make you like me for
me. I only wanted to be treated
nice as anyone would. I will
never bother anyone ever again
So you will never have to fake
nice to me while you talk and
laugh behind my back. I would
like to thank Ericka for being
nice to me. You are a good
person...

...and spanky you are fat. HA HA LOL

In Loving memory of Patty Jakes

S
R.I.P
R.I.P
R.I.P
R.I.P

22

Serveral Kids Are At the
PARK, SHARING Their stories
of being bullied.

23

I GET BODY SHAMED OFTEN
IM SICK OF PIZZA FACE BECAUSE I HAVE THESE FRECKLES
I'M CALLED HE SHE BECAUSE I HANG WITH THE GUYS
FOR SOME REASON THEY CALL ME FAT BECAUSE I'M SKINNYLY CHALLENGED
THEY CALL ME BLACK OIL BOY BECAUSE OF MY DARK SKIN
IM CALLED BOMB BOY BECAUSE I'M MUSLIM
THEY CALL ME BORDER HOPPER
THEY CALL ME POOR WHITE TRASH
24

the spoiled Bratt Girlz Are
still up to their old Bullying
ways two days After Pattys
Memorial.

25

I CAN'T BELIEVE THEM
WHAT THE FRIED PICKLES AND POPCORN IS WRONG WITH YA'LL ?
I GUESS PEOPLE JUST DON'T LEARN
DANG FOREAL
WHAT THA WHAT
BYE ILLEGAL BLACKY FATTY PIZZA FACE AND GIRL BOY.
26

ABOUT THE AUTHOR

RAYVELL A. VANN was born and raised in INGLEWOOD CALIFORNIA as a youngster I had a very deep vice like a grown man so people kids and adult would often call me froggy, a name that I hated a lot to me that was there way of bulling me so I spent a lot of time to myself so I wouldn't have to talk to people over the years its seems like it became ok to bully people that were different or less fortunate than others many kids and grownups have committed suicide because they were bullied and this needs to stop and the best way to stop it is not to let the bully win I wrote this in hopes of anyone that is a victim of bullying or knows of anyone in need of a friend to help them not get bullied will help NOT TO LET THE BULLY WIN TOGETHER WE CAN STOP BULLING I am now the father of three daughters and I like you would hate to know that my kids were a victim of a bully or would become a bully themselves . read this book and learn from it.